This is a work of fiction, the characters, incidents and dialogues are products of the author's imagination. This book is not to be construed as real or true in any short. Any resemblance to actual events or person, living or dead, is enteral coindental.

Karen the Horror Stories

Author: Andre Johnson

Contributions By: Roy F.

D.S.

Earl Lewis

Authors other books on Amazon:

Karen the Origin Story

Tedzells Poems and Short Stories

Discount Code: books

10% Off Order

https://www.etsy.com/shop/Tedzells

The Beginnings End

For as long as Noah could remember, he wanted to do something with technology. But being Amish, he knew it could never happen. Let alone with help from his sister and their two friends. The group never imaged that they would build anything with technology, let alone bio robots. Especially robots that can think like humans, look like humans, talk smoothly like humans and even be able to eat food. Because they are robots and do not need food. It was just a way to make them seem normal in public. But the hardest thing to fully accomplish was the power supply for the robots. They figured that an electricity-based power supply was a good idea at first. Then after a few failed trial runs proven it not to have a steady charge. So, a liquid base had to be the only other choose. And with the proper mixture of pumpkin spice latte, white claws, daiquiri et cetera could keep them properly running. If it cannot ingest a proper water source.

Anita, Lizzy and Jedidiah had been with him every step of this journey. But none of them can remember how they named a fleet of all female bio robots, Karen. Nonetheless Noah planned to send the bots out to different states across America. Places like Nevada, California, and New York. Well, all except Florida and Flint, Mi. This is because, it is a shit ton of crazy people already in Florida. So, there is no good reason to send any

Karen's there. There is already a lot of stupid shit happening there. For example, theme parks, tropical storms, and crocodiles on meth probably. It would have been a waste of recourse to send some there. And for Flint, MI it was because of the water supply issues. The bio robots' main source of energy came from water-based drinks like water and pumpkin spice lattes. So, the group is worried how the lead or legionnaire bacteria would mess up the bio robots.

But Noah had come up with the idea from a newspaper article he read as a child. It was about a car powered by water and the sheer accomplishment of that amazed him. Noah incorporated it into his own ideas when they discovered a factory up for sale at a good price. That an it had unlimited water supply since they were on Belle Island. A lot of the water experiments had failed. Eventually, they cracked it and the first liquid-based bio robots were invented and operational. At least he was about to find out about the last bit. The tanks hissed and smoke escaped from them simultaneously as the doors opened. Noah literally held his breath as the Karen's stepped out and approached him. "Deactivate robotic motor functions," Noah commanded as he clicked buttons on his computers, "human motor functions online." The Karen's taken to the new command and all naked. Then they began to twist and stretch their bodies like actual people. Anita came and placed a shoulder on his arm, beaming all-round. "It's magnificent Noah. Look at them!" then out of nowhere he was snapped out of a daydream by Jedidiah. That's because Jedidiah was hitting him with a pool noddle for ignoring Anita.

Anita called out again hunched over at the computer screen while everyone else walked over. "Okay. Here goes nothing," said Noah. "You mean everything." Anita interjected after a little giggle. So, with the press of a button, stuff started to happen. Lights started flashing, with strange sounds to match. And with a tone of seriousness, I think we did it? Thank all really. I didn't think we could do anything like this said Noah. Things are going right the Karen's are firing up. One small step for Amish and one bigger step for humankind. "You're not Neil Armstrong dickhead." Noah scoffed. "Hell, Neil Armstrong wishes he was me!" As they laughed, he pulled down the lever and the chain reaction started. The liquid emptied from the tanks and smoke filled the tanks.

When the tanks finally filled up with a liquid substance, the final steps would almost done. Then someone clears their throat. "Are you ready for this?" Then a figure walked slowly from the dark area of the warehouse, before coming under a light. "Anita!" Then he faced back towards the computers. Why are you so jumpy, brother? This is a great fucking day. What if it doesn't fucking work? This is basically our last chance if this doesn't work. Noah heaved as Anita placed a reassuring hand on his shoulder. "It will work; all the test runs finally went smooth. The Karen's are going to do what they are supposed to do Noah." "I hope you're right sis. I really do." Building the Karen's now became they're life's work which stood in front of them. Each one of those creations was magnificent. Expect for the test run one, which one keep getting arrested by the police.

That one Karen kept walking up and down Michigan Avenue being extra crazy. Protesting about equal pay and being able to walk around topless. But the police just though Karen is on something and is just high all of the time. But with this they also realized that they are going to have to give them some type of last name to keep track of them. So that way if they need software updates, repairs or if they can't find one. It would be easier than just typing Karen into their database to search for them. So, the group decides the robots last names would be the cities that they would be in.

"Congratulations team Amish." Jedidiah said. Then rose his glass filled with Faygo Moon Mist. "To Noah, you are fucking son of a bitch you did it!" After a small celebration they realized they left all the Karen's naked in the room. Now the Karen's were dressed and waiting for official orders. "So how quick are you integrating them?" Lizzy asked, drumming her fingers on her water bottle. "Well as soon as possible. Why waste time?" Noah said. "I mean, yeah. But that's quick?" "Anita said they are good to go. Right sis?" "Yeah." Anita replied, bringing her focus to the talk. "They're alright. You guys have outdone yourself." "We think Anita?" Jedidiah said. While playing in his beard. "Yeah, okay they're fine, just don't rub it in my face.

"What I'm saying is, is it wise to send them out to the states this early? Lizzy didn't stop tapping her glass and didn't make eye contact. Noah noticed. "What's happening here? Why are you two nervous? Anything I should know about?" Noah asked, while his facial expression is so serious. "We're not nervous. Just cautious." Are we sure we should send them to different states? I thought we talked about only getting pay back on people in Michigan for treating us badly. Jedidiah kept his gaze on the ground. "Jedidiah, are you thinking about anything I should know about?" "No." "Then great. We continue as planned. Fucking cheers." Noah dropped his glass on a table and walked away. The trio spent a moment looking at each other in silence before Anita left to join the Karen's.

Anita hoped something wasn't wrong and that the Karen's were fine. A part of her wanting to panic. The other part reminded her that there was no reason for Liz and Jed to fuck them over. Fine! As Anita walked away. While Jedidiah noticing an alert on the computer. Then Jedidiah went to check the cameras and notice tactical vehicles coming towards the factory. Then he triggered the alarms. Which for some reason the song was "Wannabe." Which activated the Karen's into party mode. Which will give the group a little distraction to get to the tunnels and escape like El Chapo.

Agent Carson jumped out of the trucks and went in formation with the SWAT team. Then they breached the front door and found some women on the main floor of the factory. It looked like they were parting to a Spice Girls soundtrack. After finding these women dancing, swat cleared the rest of the factory. After that the feds and the local police did their investigation, they concluded that these women where all hostages. They determined this because, during their investigation Agent Carson thought all the women had Stockholm syndrome. This conclusion came to be because all the women kept repeating the same things over and over. "I belong here, you can't do anything to me! And I want to speak to a supervisor!" So, after days of hearing the same things over and over, they would eventually stop looking for the people who kidnaped them. Also, they realized it would save them from the headaches and paperwork.

All while this is happening, the teens had made it back to their Amish community. Then some things went somewhat back to normal for the gang. Also, the kids where happy enough that their community accepted them back without judgement. Or for not kicking them out for explaining how there rumspringa went, because it sounds very crazy. Which at this point Noah, Anita, Lizzy and Jedidiah knew they could talk freely because no one will believe them.

Extreme Couponer Tiktoker

The Karen in Southfield

With my life being perfectly normally, I wanted to create a Tik Tok account to show people who I really am. I want to aspire them to be a better version of themselves. The concept of me making videos is because I get bored. Also, I hope that people will watch my videos and see what first world poor look like. The first video I ever made was a hair styling video. Where I talked about different random looks and how most women can look like. You must cut your hair and just some blond streaks in it to make it look really fierce. After I got my haircut for the first time, I was being treated much better everywhere I went. Other women were even asking me I got my hair done. From there it took off and now I spend every moment with my phone ready to record. Just in case something worthy comes my way.

So, I went to the park the other day like normal. There were these horrible kids playing basketball and loud music. Just doing teenager's stuff. I couldn't believe how so many adults just walked by and let this happen. I bet they were scared of those kids but not me. Then I started to think to myself, why are all these broken condoms walking around? Is lululemon having a sale? Where is the nearest coffee shop? But I just turned on my camera than walked right up to them to set them straight. This is a public park and you shouldn't be here acting like a bunch of hooligans. So, I told those whipper snappers they shouldn't be in public acting like this and should kick rocks. Everyone around you is trying to have a peaceful day. After I posted the video, I felt proud of myself. So, I bought a bottle of wine on the way home to read the comments.

I gotten random comments like how brave I am or how I am helping make the world for the better. Even the police don't do as much as I do when it comes to helping neighborhood. The other comments are all trolls and haters. I make sure to report them when they comment things. Things like mind your own business cunt nugget. Or she probably pegs her boyfriend acting like that. People say insulting stuff like this to make me feel bad. But they don't know is that they're hated fueled me even more. Plus calling someone cunt nugget is somewhat a decent insult. Some people hate using words like this because they don't want children talking like this. But I say fuck them kids.

Today so much happened to me. So much that I think I will have to break it up into a few videos. The reason why is because how good my couponing skills are. It is one of my favorite hobbies that I enjoy now. I think that I am becoming the biggest name in Southfield at couponing now. I have started so many groups to teach people things that will make sure they never pay full price for anything again. There is no reason to pay any stores marked up prices. Especially when you can just use coupons and get things for so much cheaper. I think people that pay full price are idiots and I would never be friends with them. I have made these amazing binders that I fill up every few days. Also, before a shopping trip I make a video showing all my new ones, then how much I spend. I don't go shopping without less than two binder of coupons. Also, I make fun of people that don't use coupons. Usually, it goes fine but for some reason everybody at the store decided they had to have a problem with me today is why I have so many videos to expose these horrible people. I hope that they get called out publicly for what they did to me because honestly it was a little bit traumatic for people around me. They were ganging up on me. I started to play the victim so people will leave me alone. They deserve to be exposed for what they had done to me. They need to be treated the same way and I will do so.

After a few days later, I started shopping like usual I take all the hand soap off the shelf just because I can. I used to give it all the stuff to food banks and homeless shelters. That was until I realized I keep shutting down and rebooting for being too nice. To me it's simple, nothing but chaos now. These mouth breathers just need a little inconvenience from their daily retinues for attacking me for just doing discount shopping. I had amazing deals on toilet paper, so I just filled up my cart with as much as they had. A few people started throwing fits. It doesn't make sense why people wanted more tissue because of Covid? If they wanted it so badly, they would have gotten it first instead of waiting till the middle of the day. Then another lady told me that I can't take all the baby formula because other mothers really need some also.

I knew that was a lie because if she really had a baby, she could just feed it herself without needing the formula. I just meet a lady who had a baby and I thought her how to coupon. I knew that I could sell her the formula for under market price and still make a profit off of it. I told those people phatic they should watch my videos to learn. Then they would make the most out of a trip to the store. I had everything from cleaning products to cans of tuna by the time I was ready to check out. I swear the cashier must not know what she was doing because she was going so slowly at ringing up my stuff. I have other things to do and she was just wasting my time.

I come to love handing over my coupons and seeing that huge number go down to almost nothing. But this cashier had the nerve to tell me that I couldn't use all these coupons. Which I replied angrily, shut up lint licker and get me the manager. What I want to teach people need to speak up or the world will walk all over them. Don't take "no" as an answer especially from a cashier. The manager made her ring up all my coupons while I mocked her for wasting everyone time. When I left I saw the huge line behind me and these people looked mad at me like I was the issue. If there is a problem, it's not mines.

If I am going to spend my money than everyone can wait. One woman even called me a dick and I think her child was saying cootie queen or something. Then I told that random lady, if she walked other than using an electric scooter she would not be fat. She was probably just jealous that her bill wasn't going to be cheap like mines. At that point I made sure on my way out to grab a bunch more coupons. Just to spite them even more. One comment I get a lot is, what do I do with all the money that I save with my couponing. I think that is a great question and I think that it is important to treat yourself after you do all that hard work. I replied with buying more white claws and minding my own business.

Every week I give a garage update video showing all the excess stuff I got from my couponing adventures. Even those videos get trolls saying I should give the things away to people that need it. If people needed it that badly they would get a job and make the money to earn it. Couponing is not that hard especially because I'm doing it to make people angry. Randomly I got a transmutation on updates today. The newest one said I needed to drink different types of liquids other than white claws and pumpkin spice. This finally came clear to me after waiting almost a half an hour waiting for a latte and being ok with it. So, after a long day of couponing I didn't want to cook, so I went out to eat. I decided that I would just order the salad with salmon on it. The cook wanted to make a whole big deal about it "not being on the menu".

They had salmon on the menu, and they had salad on the menu. All they had to do was put some salmon on the salad and it would have been easy. I finally got it after telling then the customer is always right. They decided they were going to charge me more just because I came in fifteen minutes before closing time. Again, I had to call the manager but this time he backed up his waiter and told me that I was going to have to pay what they told me. He didn't even offer me a free dessert from the harassment and rudeness I got. This was supposed to be my time to relax but instead I got attacked by this horrible wait staff. I am going to leave a bad review on Yelp and make sure to tell my followers to never go eat there because they don't respect their customers.

I think I need to make a series of TikTok's talking about how people harass me in public because of my standards. I swear they act like this on purpose just because they think it's funny to watch me get upset. I swear when I see other people pulling out their phones, I make sure to tell them they don't have my permission to post a video of me online. I look at a ton of videos on TikTok every night and make sure that I am not in any of them. I haven't seen any yet but if I do, I am going to sue whoever put them up without asking. The only good thing is it gives me a ton of content for my page. I know that all my real fans love and support everything that I do. I am an icon for women out there and no matter what these trolls say to me I am never going to stop being who I am. Were meant to make the world much worse.

Wine Vineyards

The Karen in Grand Rapids

Fubar's Vineyard is known for its very expensive array of wines. However, not a single person ever left Fubar's vineyard sober or disappointed. This is because the quality and quantity of the wine given. The customer service, however, left a lot to be desired. Especially being in Grand Rapids where the city best known for its breweries and normal dive bars. This was mainly because it is a college town and brewery area. Nonetheless customers enjoyed experience with every visit.

This was quickly negated after the notorious Assistant Manager Eleanor Stoddart had her baby. Eleanor made the place what it was and that's what people come back again and again. But because she just had a baby the manger gave her maternity leave surprisingly. The manger hired a temp assistant manager which was Karen. Karen GR was well knowledge on this company history by downloading the company info page to her main frame. Plus, a generic history from google about running a wine vineyard and the history of all wines. It helps doing certain things when knowing most things.

Karen GR believed herself to be the sommelier of this town. All the people fortunate enough to work shifts with Karen GR hated it so much. But were too afraid to tell her that she neither owned the vineyard, nor the wine produced from it. Karen GR was working her normal early morning shift when a customer came in to look at which wines were available for purchase. Just from how the lady was dressed, Karen GR. disliked her immediately. This customer had comfortable brown boots, with faded jeans and a wool hoodie on. Karen GR. was jealous of the lady's brunette hair, tied into a ponytail. Although Karen GR never felt this type of emotion before. Would never admit to being so but wasn't built that way. She only had scruffy, dirty blonde hair cut short, above the shoulders. "Hello?" The lady called out to the seemingly empty shop floor. Karen GR. Was skulking from around the corner, just out of sight, but she strode out to meet the lady to keep her from waiting.

"Hello," Karen GR. Said with a curt smile, "welcome to Fubar's Vineyard, how may we be of service to you today? "HI," the lady said, smiling, "I'm in a little bit of a hurry. Do you have any red wine available in bulk for purchase? I'm hoping to get a couple of bottles for the party I'm throwing." "Well, I'm sorry that you're in a *bit of a hurry*," Karen said with a slight snort of derision, "we do try to be as efficient as we can. I *apologies* if that doesn't meet your lofty standards." "I'm sorry, have

I done something to offend you?" "Not at all," Karen GR said while her face twisting into a sickly smile. It would be understandable to mistake such a smile with a sneer or a snarl, too. "I'd just like to buy some wine and be on my way," the lady said, "if that isn't any trouble?" "No trouble. None." Karen GR went off to find some of the bottles that she knew was going bad. The lady waited patiently for Karen GR to return.

"I'm so *sorry* for your wait," Karen GR said. As she came back with two bottles of red wine then placed them on the counter to begin the sale. Can I just buy these and leave? The lady asked. What do you think I'm doing? While pointing at the till. A bit of patience goes a long way. Then Karen decided to make the women more flustered. Sorry mama this establishment has a new rule here. One of them is we can't give out more than two bottles to go to one customer. You know what? Then the lady snapped, I think I'm going to go and take my business elsewhere. You've been a horrible person this entire time. The lady stormed out of the store and Karen GR. Sneered as she left. Now she could go back to doing what she did best. Managing an empty store. At least until the manger figures it out and fires me.

A Flat Earthier Christen

The Karen in Taylor

Opinions are something that everyone has and should say out loud a lot. But sometimes, some people cannot understand to accept that others have different views. Karen T is one of those people that didn't understand this concept. She had many opinions that she liked sharing and one of her "controversial" ones was "flat earth". She was always a believer and couldn't understand how others had different opinions about it. Another essential thing to know about Karen was that she believed herself to always be right. She always tried convincing others to believe that her beliefs were the right ones, and she was very annoyed about it. The usual people targeted is neighbors and delivery people. So random conversation always started on site. "As I told you yesterday, it's impossible for the Earth to be round," Karen T said. "Not round, but ellipsoid," replied Kyle. "What are you talking about? You don't even know what that word means," she replied angrily.

"It's a shape," Kyle said smiling. That Earth being flat makes way more sense. How could the Earth be just a ball floating in space? she asked. "So, what? It's like a plate?" asked Kyle. That's the moment when Karen usually gets angry and leaves.

Kyle was used to having that conversation almost every day, as Karen T was trying to convince him. She explained to everyone that the Earth was flat, but most people didn't even listen to her. But then, things got even more complicated, when Karen T started going to church. After one of her neighbors invited her to their church. She started liking it and going constantly. The main reason was downloading all the different types of bibles to her main frame. After a while Karen T realize people caused a lot of trouble with these books all across the world. And like usually, Karen started acting crazy like church people just to piss everyone off.

She stopped wearing make-up, removed her earrings and started wearing only long dresses. She started carrying a bible with her everywhere. Just to convince everyone that religion was the way. Her first real fight was with a Karen that came with her. It was about how they both have the same name and who will have to change names. Why are you so quiet? You normally give some type of feedback. Finally, the other Karen replied. I was only thinking of a different name I can use to keep our cover. I would like to be called Becky from now on and you can keep the name of Karen. You can stay with thing of being a flat earthier believer that's a christen now. And I will be your sister who go to expos and fan convention to piss people off.

Right after they agreed Karen T comment you're exaggerating angrily. But out of nowhere Becky heard music and fun coming from outside? Karen then asked is someone having fun outside. Why do they need this?" said Karen. Having fun is a sin and they are leading these children to hell. And also, for you all believing the earth being round. She replied smiling. Karen, stop! Kyle yelled. I won't stop; these things need to be heard. Your children will be stupid and sinful because of stuff like this, Karen shouted. Where going to need you to leave, we don't want you here, go home! I'm the only one here who's trying to save you and your children, and you just ignore me? You people trying to send me home? Outside is a free place, ha!

Please Karen, stop this and go home, said Kyle, begging her. All the children are listening to you fight with the you people. While all this is happening, Becky is on the porch hyping her sister up. Saying pointless things that was making the neighbors even more frustrated. Things like, how can we take you serous sir your wife is taller than you. Or we won't listen to you especially when your kids don't. But the one that made Karen laugh. You can't wear white after Labor Day that is a sin. You're insane. And let me tell you something I never wanted to, Karen said, taking a deep breath, you're so annoying, and self-centered that it's crazy. It would be very easy to target people at place like this. Everyone is allowed to have an opinion and live their lives believing whatever they want. You have no right to coming out here and preach religion to everyone epically other people children, Kyle added. You lecture about free will, and believing what you want, doing what you want. But you are wrong because what you say out loud might get you in trouble Kyle shouted. Karen replied calmly. Arrogance and pride are also form of sinning.

And that's when they decide to walk back into the house. She didn't like others calling her out on her mistakes. But when they both made it back in the house, Karen decided to call the police. She called about drunk people in public and around kids. A few days past and most of the people forgot about what had happen. But not Karen T, she was still focused. But the only difference now is that she will not have backup from Becky this time. It's because Becky went to some comic con for some super hero movie that's coming out. Becky seemed happy before leaving because she doesn't have to hide being a robot. Also, everyone that goes to these types of events are easy targets to upset. Nonetheless Karen still had a mission to do but needed a boost of energy.

So, a trip to the local coffee shop she went. After leaving the coffee shop Karen felt a little bit happier. So, she decided to enjoy the decent weather and take a walk to the park. Especially when she was double fisting hot chocolate and people watching. While sitting on a bench, Karen noticed Kyle then went to say hello. After he notice it was her, he snapped. Stop telling everyone about a flat earth and forcing religion on others. No one cares, Kyle shouted. But you just agreed with me somewhat," said Karen, confused. I lied; you are a horrible woman? shouted Kyle.

Lying is a sin, a sin. You're deeper in hell with every lie. Careful not to reach the end, she said, bitterly. "I promise that I won't. You know why? Because that's where you'll be while smiling and walking away. At this point Karen realized she now needed new tactics. So, she created a group called "flat religion." Where they talk about both a flat Earth and God. She was hosting it in the church and managed to gather a hand full of people. But she lost almost everybody after the first meeting. After trying to convince them all that they were going to hell. After this Karen started preaching and fighting with people about her opinions everywhere. At the church, in stores, and sometimes in traffic. Nonetheless she continued to preach, no matter how many times people told her to stop.

The Repairs

Now that the Karen's are fully operation, there's a bigger issue the workers have to deal with. The dilemma for the Karen repair group is how, to find the things needed for the repairs needed. This was because every so often, the Karen's would need software updates or repairs. The Bay City Karen needs a new arm and skin from the shoulder down. She was playing with deer's during hunting season and was hit with an arrow. The Karen in Graying went for a walk in the woods. Not knowing she was on the military base, then got blown up by the engineers using demo. Another Karen near Lake Superior wanted to be a fish. After seeing all the sea creatures, she wanted to be one of them. All these unforeseen circumstances would normally be horrible. But this good intel for the software updates and to let the other Karen's know what to beware of.

Normally after a Karen get repaired, a function check required. Then after its completer they go back to their respected cities. Now that they can't use the factory equipment the new way is to go to a club. This group went hand in hand as they walk the streets of the downtown area. This group jokes and laughs like they known each other forever. Mostly about how Karen S thinks she better than everyone else. The Karen's that was repaired were out and about. It felt like a perfect moment to bond for them. The main thing they figured out was that they were create by Amish teens. Also, the ridiculousness is that they get repaired by other robots. That and each one has special trait to make them seems more human.

Like Karen T could roll her tongue. Karen S could bend her thumb backwards. Then Karen M could escape handcuffs like she had no bones. They found a random bar on Woodward that was having a karaoke night. They would attempt to sing songs. Songs like Wrecking Ball, Let It Go and Protect Ya Neck. While Karen M telling everyone, who listen that they do over the pants stuff. While at the club they implement different types of testing like dancing, taking shots and singing. All these types of tests are to see if they were fixed properly. Finally. Somewhere relatively quiet. Karen GR said after ordering shots for her and the others at the bar. "If you call this quiet," said Karen S said.

Don't forget we have stuff to do said Karen GR. While looking at her more seriously. What do you mean? Coming from the end of the bar Karen M on her forth white claw. I mean hood rat shit, I don't know. Go on Karen S replied as she took the shots from the bartender. Cheers! Cheers Karen S while having a random head twitch. So, do you think maybe I'm malfunctioning or. Then her voice trailed off. Karen GR squeezed her face after taking the shots and they laughed when she said she might need liquid to quench her throat. Then she spoke more seriously. No, I felt the same way too and I don't know. What's happening? Could it be a malfunction? Who's going to do a system check?

Moments after that, the results came up on their phones. Then they were stopped by the software Karen. The software Karen told them what the real issues with them was. If it is more than two Karen's at the same place for more than a few days a lime wire virus will be activated. It was programed that way into their systems, so if something ever happened protocols are in place. So, in the morning everyone must return back to wear they came from.

Granny No

The Karen in Monroe

This story begins with an old grumpy lady, living in a calm Monroe neighborhood. She is one of the newest people to move into this gated community the past year. Even though she is kind of a nice lady, but something is very annoying about her. Karen M has her own rules that she tries to apply to anyone that lives around her. Some of the rules are not understandable and Karen is just crazy. So, let me tell you something she loves and something she hates. She absolutely loves listening to the Wu-Tang Clan while knitting. She spends her days on the porch or at the park knitting. But the thing she hates the most is people and their driving abilities. She might act crazy from time to time but don't care. Karen anger gets worse when she notices when cars are not parked right, or loud music is playing. But, this story is about how she managed to combine boredom and anger issues to create something more interesting.

As she like sitting at the park every other day knitting. She started noticing how many squirrels and birds going up to people. She started feeding them and actually developing a nice friendship with the creatures. She would feed them like any normal old person. And so, the animals started bringing her things in return. Things like little twigs, or anything else that they find. But then there was an idea formed in Karen's head; she was going to use the animal's help do bald head hood rat shit. She started training the animals little by little. Eventually they would attack people and damaged their cars on demand. And as soon as someone parked, the squirrels and birds were paying attention. If you wouldn't straighten their cars. The birds would drop an assortment of stuff. Junk like rocks, sticks, nuts or worse themselves. And the squirrels would throw nuts, or even try to scratch your car. When something like that happened, most of the drivers would just leave. Most of the drivers would just drive away, finding another parking spot.

Karen M was finally found fulfillment. As she would be knitting, she could watch the animals do their jobs. But one day, she realized that she could teach them even more. Karen started teaching the animals to steal. They would sneak through people car windows and steal anything they could grab. Then bring any items back to Karen wherever she was siting. Or the park bench she would sit. At first none of the neighbors didn't really notice. The animals were very sneaky and stole without being seen most times; But if someone saw them, they didn't really assume someone thought them. But, one day, one of Karen's neighbors saw how squirrels enter people's cars. The driver would have opened windows and started shouting to scare the squirrel. But then the squirrel would jump through the window and grabbed the person's phone then leave. The driver left, fearing that the squirrel might bring its friends. Then squirrel ran onto Karen's porch to deliver the phone.

But Karen did make one friend out of all of this nonsense. It was the local homeless drunk she saw him at the park one day. Everyone just thought he was drunk every day. That's why they thought they could understand him. All expect Karen. Karen could understand what dirty mike was talking about. That's because dirty mike knew how to speak was jive and usually talked to himself like this. Dis weada' be ho'rible man. 'S coo', bro. Global warmin' be sucka's and guv'ment be behind all uh dis. And he would get strange looks from everyone walking by him. But since he became friends with Karen, he has someone to talk to now. And it was always normal the same conversation every other day.

Hey Karen, wuts goin' on? Nodin' much Dirty Mike. What it is, Mama. Right On! Just tryin' t'get dese birds t'sucka's likes no'mal. ah' betta' protect mah' neck den. 'S coo', bro. ah' hear ya' listenin' t'Ghost Face Killa today. Slap mah fro. Right On! said Dirty Mike. What it is, Mama. Right On! What about ya' Dirty Mike, any plans today? de usually get pickled and sucka's watch. Want some booze t'go wid yo' scag today? uh course ah' do danks replied karen. 'S coo', bro. How long ya' been out here knittin' today? asked Dirty Mike. What it is, Mama. Right On! about an hour and some few dozen scags. What ya' been doin' today Mike? ah' been at da damn shelta' ova' laplaisance rd, tryin' t'get mah' life right. right on. 'S coo', bro. And they would just like to be in each other's company.

Nonetheless whenever the squirrels or birds would ever do something for Karen they would get paid in treats. A neighbor saw the whole thing play out one day. So, he decided to look more closely at whatever was happening. He would find little tasks to do outside every day. Just so he can watch Karen and the creatures doing. He noticed how the animals would attack cars without a single word from her. He also noticed that they didn't attack all the cars. Then he started being interested in the why. It took him about a week to see what the whys was. He went outside one day to test his theory with his own car. As soon as he pulled up with loud music and parked wrong then went in his house.

Is Then birds started to crash into the window, hitting it with their beak. He opened the door and started making random noise. And that's when the few squirrels ran off un different direction not to get caught. He then saw one squirrel run straight to the woman, in disappointment. The man came out of his house and went to comfort the woman. Karren was knitting, enjoying some coffee obviously, unbothered and calm. I'm sorry, this might sound stupid, but did you train these squirrels? he asked. No, I just feed them, she replied without even looking at the man. They just seem to react to a pattern, to have a certain routine. And that routine somehow profits you, he replied.

That's simply not true, she said, now if you are nice enough, let me finish this nice beanie I started, she added. The man laughed as he saw his watch right next to the women's coffee, but he didn't say anything. He left and thought of the correct way to handle the situation. So, he started gathering proof of what he was suspecting. He started taking photos of the animals attacking the cars and people. Also, how they would sneak into the cars and steal stuff. Most importantly how they took the things to the woman. He took all of those to the police and explained everything. And then, the police started investigating that too. They went undercover into the neighborhood and doing all the stuff the neighbor told them about. They proved that what the man was saying was true and so they went to talk with Karen. We need you to come down to the station with us said one of the policemen. Why is that? Is knitting a crime? Karen said, trying to keep a straight face.

It's not, but unfortunately for you, we found out that you are an evil zoologist of some sort. We are aware of how of how you control the squirrel's and birds, said the policeman. Officer, how could I do that? They're animals, they do whatever they want, Karen replied. But you trained them, didn't you? Trained them to attack people and cars that don't park straight. Then steal from those cars, if possible, another policeman said. Sounds like an amazing fictional story, but that's impossible, she replied. The police, tired of her mocking them, entered her house and searched it. They found a lot of the neighbor's things. Like phone chargers, jewelry, hair ties and wallets. They threatened Karen with jail time if she didn't return everyone stuff. She didn't have to spend a lot of time in handcuffs. That's because decides to pay the fines. was enough for her to learn a lesson. So that's what they thought. They didn't do enough research on Karen M. Karen M goes city to city to do the same thing.

A Protester

The Karen in Oak Park

I remember the first time I met a vegan person. Or rather, on what they had brought to that frozen food shelf. I wanted to buy my beloved frozen meat lovers pizza of course. But I was in a hurry that day have made a very big mistake. When I went to go make my food that evening, after a hard day of doing nothing. The packaging looked a bit different than usual. It had a green border, but I didn't think anything of it. Packaging changes all the time and at least it said "Meat Lovers" on the box. I turned up the oven and took it out of its plastic wrapping. It also looked a bit different than usual. The meat on it looked different, paler and more loveless. I hated the taste of the pizza more than I hate the taste of black licorice. Again, I was puzzled, but maybe I had just caught a bad production line. I put the pizza in the oven and waited eagerly. I was really hungry. After all, I hadn't eaten since breakfast. Which was only a delicious leftover hamburger from last night dinner.

Finally, it was time. But I recoiled at the first bite. It tasted different; the meat was tough. Now I was puzzled and had a horrible taste in my mouth. There was a small "V" on the box. Emblazoned on the back was the description "vegan meat lovers". I couldn't believe my eyes and threw the whole pizza away in anger. What did that company think they were doing, offering such a thing in their store? Why would they call this thing a meat lover? So, my first encounter with something vegan nutrition understandably didn't go well. I suddenly had to watch what I bought. I had to check if my food was labelled with that damn "V". It seemed silly and incomprehensible. But I hate being healthy. More and more I noticed how the world around me was changing. Strange alternatives appeared on the menus. Tofu and all that rubbish stuff.

They were slowly replacing my beloved fatty foods with lookalike that are vegan. I also watched in horror as vegan burger restaurant opened. That's anti-Amish just like Canada bacon. That was the last straw for me. I am not upset with new business opening up but they should not trick people with crap like this. If no one was going to do anything, then I had to do something. I searched the internet for allies and quickly found them. Meat lovers just like me. People were equally dismayed false advertising. Some of my friends encouraged me to try. I didn't want to try vegan or vegetarian food. It's against my religion. Who would do this to their body.

These militant vegans were trying to force their lifestyle on everyone. So, I decided that I had to make my stand. After a few weeks of fighting against all vegans and vegetarians, I found a notice about a vegan street food festival. The perfect place to finally demonstrate against this nonsense. I made a sign and buttons. Someone had shirts made, with roast beef picture on the front of it. Everyone in the group liked them. Also, on the back it said, Sponsored by xHamster. Another person brought a big bucket of chicken wing before we ventured near the festival. Of course, I had fortified myself sufficiently beforehand, because you couldn't eat anything at this event anyway. And it was worse than I had expected. Instead of fatty foods. There were booths everywhere with "vegan hamburger", "vegan steak" or "vegetarian bratwurst". How could they deface our food culture like this? At least I could have understood vegetables and fruit. But this disgrace? This was going too far.

I stood demonstratively next to one of the booths with my sign and ate my chicken wings in peace. The first looks I got were confused, but soon this turned into hatred. Of course, I didn't miss the opportunity to make some comments about the booth next to me. "Well, wouldn't you rather go on eating some grass? You end up eating my food anyway!" At first, my sentences were ignored.

Which I found quite rude. But eventually, a young man with long blond hair came up to me. He was thin, probably due to the malnutrition he was putting himself through. I would walk around trying to hand out high calorie foods.

"People, don't you want some of our chicken wings? You're all pale already. You really need to eat animal meat protein so you don't pass out!" "Sir, I'm sorry, but I'm going to have to ask you to stand somewhere else. You're putting off our customers and frankly, your behavior is a bit of an overreach!" I laughed. Some random boy didn't have a clue of what was happen at all. "Your behavior is encroaching. You interfere in my life and want to tell me what to eat! And now you want to tell me where to stand as well? This is not how we bet!" The blond man, who had been smiling uncertainly before, turned a little paler. "But sir, I really just want to ask them to stand somewhere else!" "What else? Are you going to hit me? Turn me in? This is a free country, I can stand where I want and express my opinion!" The young man looked at me helplessly. He didn't seem to have the courage to contradict me. Maybe he also secretly wanted some of my chicken wings and was just too powerless to say anything. He shrugged and left, muttering something unintelligible under his breath. I considered that a success. That same evening, I looked for a new event to boycott. I would find local allies and until then it was my personal mission.

Alternative Ending

"People, don't you want some of my chicken wings? You're all pale already. You really should eat some protein so you don't fall off the meat!" However, the young man just smiled and shook his head. "Thank you, sir, but I actually just wanted to offer them something for free. We have some chicken wings made from seitan at our stall as well. They're boneless, of course, but you might enjoy them!" He pulled out a bucket of vegan things. They looked frighteningly real, something that made me angry right back. "If you want to go "vegan", why are you imitating my beloved meat?" I asked angrily. "Most of us actually like meat. We just don't want to create animal suffering, so we try vegan alternatives. You don't have to try these, but I'm happy to offer them again" I glanced at the bucket and smelled it briefly. It didn't smell repulsive, at least. I shook my head anyway but became thoughtful. "Maybe one day they'll be ready. Why don't you come back next time? You can still do the free tasting then!" The young man moved away and I looked after him thoughtfully. How much did the chickens really have to suffer for my chicken wings? Was this really true? I left the event, and my chicken wings no longer tasted so good that day.

Conspiracy Theory

Joan puts down her eyeglasses and relaxed into her reclining chair. She couldn't believe how long she had been absolved into the plan at hand. While she sees herself as a normal human doing the normal thing to improve the world simply by following her grandfather's desire. Others saw her as the Devil incarnate that was trying so hard to lopsided the balance of the world at hand. The whole dream started as soon as she was in growing up in her mother's womb. Finally, it was placed in her hands to continue and achieve the results. Her paternal grandfather raised her father the Amish way.

No, they all weren't born Amish. In fact, she came from a most American family, although her paternal grandmother was Amish. It seemed as though her grandpa got so stricken and had fallen so much in love with her grandma that he was ready to accept her way of life fully as his own. A well-known politician and businessman, he wanted everyone else to see the world through his lens. Or could it be that the philosophical and religious part of him gave way to his plans? He raised his kids as Amish and made sure everyone else in the family followed suit. Now coming down to his plans, all grandpa wanted was to imbibe the Amish way in every other person just like he had done to his family.

Joan's father knew the way and now that he was dead. She had to uphold that particular way. Not only must she uphold it, but she must also extend the knowledge and allow it spread about the world or die trying. How did she plan on going about it? The only thing her father figures had were ideas, they didn't know the exact way they wanted to go about it. If Joan was brought up to be outspoken like any other westernized child. s\She would have told them they only had ideas in their heads and had no way to bring them to life. She would openly call them stupid and unready. But Joan didn't need all that; instead she was going to breathe life into her plans. She knew she could get the work to see the open path and benefits of adapting to the Amish culture of life. Her phone rang suddenly, "Ma'am, we have the official representative of the president on call. Should I transfer the call to you?" It was her secretary. "Yeah. Sure. Remember, we have been waiting for this all along."

"Yes, ma'am. Right away." Joan tapped her perfectly trimmed nails against the furniture as two beeps sounded and a raspy voice flowed through the speakers. "What a pleasant day, Joan." She and the president's representative had exchanged words a few numbers of times as he tried to persuade her to rethink her choices and offers. To be frank, they do not like each other's guts. "I would have said the same but I do not lie," Joan said. "Yeah, right." She could feel him roll his eyes. "Your religion does not permit you to." "I see you are in a rather odd mood so can we get straight to the point? How is the president feeling towards my suggestions? Has an agreement been closed?" She asked. There was no response for about a minute. Joan looked at the screen of her phone, then the voice spoke again, "Yes, we have. There is absolutely no choice. We have to keep all of humanity." "Perfect," Joan said in a clipped tone although she could almost not hide the excitement in her voice. It was a proud moment for Joan. Even though she could only celebrate the moment with her secretary and workers. It still made her happy that she had established the lifelong dreams of her family.

The president of the country in agreement with the head of the health organizations has accepted that everyone be indoctrinated. Every human on earth without any exception would be Amish. Joan could imagine life making sense again. Parents would be able to establish respect with their kids while kids will remain disciplined and respectful to every figure of authority. There would be a beginning of internet censorship to being the use of the internet under control. If she was to follow her grandpa's footsteps to the core, she would have banned the entire use of modern technology but to be honest, the world is really nothing without technology. The best to do was control the media and that would be her first action to take. Joan knew how badly her identity had been pasted on every news media, blog, website, you name it. She was the talk of extremism and she wondered if at times she was.

Thinking back to years ago when she was still young in the fight. Her father had been caught 'spearheading a conspiracy group', that was why he had gone under the radar. He abandoned everything that had to do with grandpa and their goals. Joan wasn't like him, she wasn't a quitter, and she was her grandpa's protégé. Unlike many others born into the religion, Joan is a renowned scientist that experimented on diseases and found cures for them.

She had devoted over 20 years of her life to the cause and miraculously, the world needed her. Despite the theories going about that she and other scientists that believed in her. The way of life might have exposed the world to an extremely deadly disease just so people could turn to her as their next savior, it wasn't so. It was just a mix of unfortunate incidents that happened to fall in her favor. Her hard work resulted in finding a cure a few years after.

Now that she had what the world wanted, she wanted to engage the world in a trade by barter arrangement. Law cases had been brought up against her and Joan hardly went out during the day. There would always be someone lurking somewhere to hit her with an egg or worse, shoot her right in the skull. How could the world be so against an action that would benefit all? The Amish Church is a blessed one that believed in love, cooperation, and family. A culture built solidly on assigning roles and duties to every single individual in the family for the purpose of progress and productivity. Joan knows for certain that bringing in friends and family is the bedrock of partnership. People can now work hand in hand to achieve goals and bring their neighbors' dreams to live by offering helping hands.

The Amish are known to believe in order also known as Ordnung. That is separating chores and tasks based on gender. Marriages are bound to last longer when the epidemic of short-lived marriage is curtailed. Since the Amish are used to having the Rumspringa which is the period that youth and adolescents, in general, begin to court. Another part of the culture that Joan holds close to her heart is the dressing aspect. The Amish are bred to dress up in the most decent and humblest way possible. The ladies have dresses as long as their calves and capes to go while the males dress in shirts; all looking plain and simply. An example is Joan herself; one wouldn't find her in alarming bright clothes, not short clothes. Joan knows she has more adjustments to make so that cohabiting with the new converts or non-Amish would be easier for all parties. While the people that were unwilling to be converted to the culture try to live their normal lives, they still had to the laid down rules and set down protocols without breaching or denouncing their own beliefs. She knew rebellions will arise. Although for the best part of it, the world would be in order. She has agreed to release the cure immediately after the documents are signed and she had been allowed to appoint her own people in power for distributing the medication and sensitizing the people on the dos and don'ts of the Amish people.

Given an estimate of five years, the whole world would be cured. Everyone would be living according to the rightful standard of the Amish Church and once again, order could remain in the land. Also, Joan could finally gain reparations for how her people were forced to serve during the war, pay taxes. Also discriminated against many years ago. She was going to bring law and order once and for all. The call ended after hashing out the arrangement with the president's representative. She felt they should be grateful she wasn't interfering with political matters such as elections and voting rights. Joan stepped out of her office with a bold smile on her face. She watched her employees scramble around to showcase their hard work and she kept walking. Joan chose to ignore them because she knew their idleness would be over once the announcement was made in a few seconds. Standing by the main gate of her research building, she counted along with the clock, 3 2 1.

Made in the USA
Monee, IL
12 December 2022

21326959R00028